MW00761099

To Mom

We love you and appreciate all you do for us everyday.

Theodore Down Under
(Australian Adventures)

Australian Children's Book

I was on my way to Australia, **the land down under**. I'd never been on a plane before so I was really excited. Looking out the window and flying through the soft, fluffy clouds was fantastic.

I'm keen to share my **adventure** with you in this book. Hopefully you **learn** some stuff about Australia too!

WoW! How do I describe what I saw? We jumped onto an enormous white boat and sailed into the ocean. The boat anchored in water that was crystal clear and you could see the bottom. Talk about cool!

Snorkelling was amazing! I saw fish, coral, clams and even a turtle. This area is part of the **Great Barrier Reef** which is one of the **Seven Wonders of the World.**

The Australian outback is amazing. This adventure took me into the middle of Australia to Uluru, also known as Ayers Rock. It is one of the biggest rocks in the world.

Trying to make a boomerang come back was hilarious and also a great souvenir to take home with me.

Learning to play the **digeridoo** was so funny. Not as simple as just blowing into it. You have to breathe in through your nose, puff out your cheeks while blowing into it with soft lips.

How's that for confusing? So much to remember and do all at once but when the sound starts coming out it's so cool!

I've seen pictures of the **Sydney Opera House** in books and on the internet but seeing it in person was awesome. It opened in 1973 and took 14 years to build.

I was so happy to take my own photo of it to show everyone back home.

Near the opera house is **Sydney Harbour Bridge**. It took 8 years to build and was opened in 1932.

Climbing the bridge was so scary but a great thing to do. When I reached the top there was a fantastic view!

Bondi Beach is one of the most famous beaches around Sydney so I had to have a surf there. The sun was out and the waves were clean so this little bear had a relaxing day out.

A T.V. show called **Bondi Rescue** has also been filmed at this beach. Maybe you can watch it!

Meeting my cousin Bella was fantastic. She talks funny and it was great just listening to her **Aussie accent**. Bella also taught me some Aussie slang which I'm going to remember and use when I get home. There are a heap of **funny words** but these were my favorites.

arvo	–	afternoon
brekky	–	breakfast
dodgy	–	bit suspicious
footy	–	Australian rules football
g'day	–	hello
mate	–	friend
rug up	–	dress warmly

Australians love their **barbeques**. I threw some shrimps on the barbie and chucked on a couple of snags, in other words, barbequed some prawns and sausages. I wanted to try some real Aussie foods so I ate.......

Meat pie and sauce – meat in a pastry with ketchup on top.......very tasty.
Pavlova – meringue with cream and fruit on top (mine had strawberries)......delicious.
Vegemite – don 't want to talk about that one.......yuk.

Two animals were on my 'must see' list, the **koala** and **kangaroo**. Lots of people think that Australians have them as pets.

Hate to be the bearer of bad news but they are only found in the bush or in the zoo which is where I saw them. I couldn't wait to get my picture taken cuddling a koala.

There are some other really cool animals in Australia. Deciding which ones were the cutest was really hard.

I loved the **wombat** which is a cute, brown furry little creature and the **platypus** that is found in rivers. It has a big, long beak. The **emu** was really funny too. It tried to eat my lunch but I was too fast for it!

Trying to kick a **footy** was so very, very hard.
The Aussies seem to be very keen on
Australian Rules Football.

They can bounce, handball and kick the footy while throwing themselves at the player with the ball. It's a crazy game but looks like loads of fun.

A creepy fact..................Australia has some of the world 's deadliest spiders and snakes.

There are a couple of creatures that I have to mention. The two deadly spiders are the redback and the funnel web. Also the brown snake is the one you don 't want to meet. Luckily **I never saw** any of them!

How 's this for a bit of trivia? There are around **24 million** people living in Australia but there are nearly 4 times that many **sheep**.

Australia is so big and with so much land there is a lot of places for sheep.

Well, every great adventure has to finish and every story must come to an end.

Hope you loved sharing mine and learnt a few things about Australia along the way.

See ya fromTheodore.

Theodore's Adventure Series

Also...

Other educational books written by us

Made in the USA
Middletown, DE
09 April 2021